First published by Parragon in 2011

Parragon
Chartist House
15-17 Trim Street
Bath BA1 1HA, UK
www.parragon.com

Written by Peter Bently
Illustrated by Deborah Melmon
Designed by Rachael Fisher
Edited by Rachel Worgan
Production by Richard Wheeler

ISBN 978-1-4454-5741-3

Printed in China

# Bunny ♥♥
# Loves
## to
# Read

## PaRRagon

Bath • New York • Singapore • Hong Kong • Cologne • Delhi
Melbourne • Amsterdam • Johannesburg • Auckland • Shenzhen

Buster Bunny loved books.

He read stories of princes...

and pirates...

and witches, and wizards...

One day, Buster's friends came over.
"Hi Buster!" they said. "Are you coming out to play?"
"Sure," said Buster with a smile, "when I've finished my book. It's all about pirates!"

"You've always got your nose in a book!" said his sister Bella.

"HOpscOtch is much more fun!"

"Books are boring!" croaked Francine.

"Why read books when you can play leapfrog?"

"Reading is not as much fun as racing each other," agreed Max.

"Don't listen to them, Buster," said Sam.
"I think books are the best!"
"Really?" asked Buster.
"Yes," said Sam, smiling. "Books are the best—

—for nibbling!"
"Hey!" laughed Buster.

Nibble!

Then Bella said, "Come on, let's leave Buster with his dumb old books and play outside!"

But it was raining. The friends looked out the window gloomily.

"Why don't you read some of my books?" asked Buster, bringing out a big box.

"We don't want to look at books," said Sam grumpily. "We're only waiting for the rain to stop."

Buster took a book out of the box. "There's a big thunderstorm in this story," said Buster. "It's all about pirates hunting for buried treasure."

"Buried treasure?" asked Sam. "Like nuts and acorns? Yum!"

"Not exactly,"
replied Buster.
"But it's very exciting.
Take a look."
"I guess there's nothing
better to do," sighed Sam.

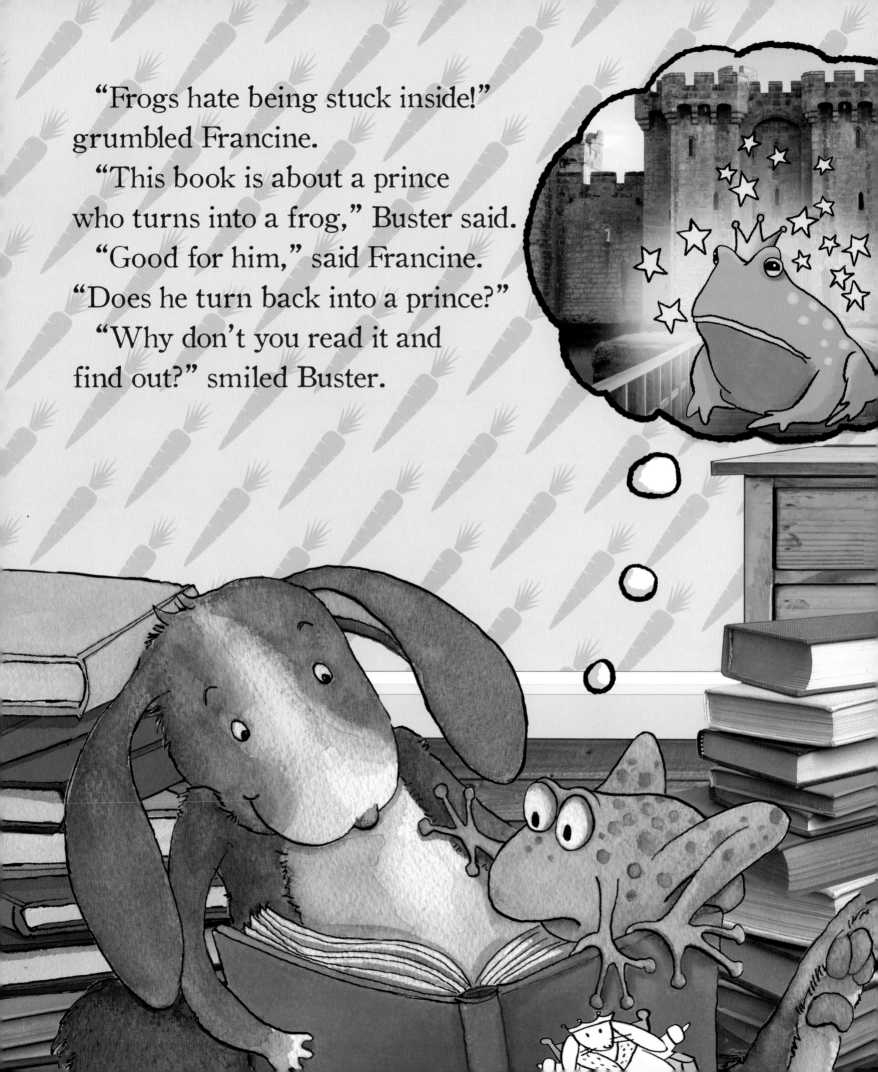

"Frogs hate being stuck inside!" grumbled Francine.

"This book is about a prince who turns into a frog," Buster said.

"Good for him," said Francine. "Does he turn back into a prince?"

"Why don't you read it and find out?" smiled Buster.

"Being cooped up inside is making me sleepy," said Max. Buster gave Max a book. "The princess in this story goes to sleep for 100 years!" he said.
"Really? WoW! How does she wake up?"
"Read it and see!" said Buster.
"Well, okay, but I might fall asleep before I finish it!"

"I'm bored! I'm going to get a cookie," said Bella.
"Hey, Buster, your box is in my way!"
"Can't you just step over it?"
"Only if I take a giant step," said Bella.

"Just like a dinosaur!"
said Buster.
"Some of them were
**bigger** than a **house!**"

"So what do you want to play?" asked Buster when the friends had all finished reading. "Hopscotch? Leapfrog? Tag?"

"Let's pretend we can do magic spells. If you give me a kiss, I'll turn into a princess!" said Francine.

"Ugh! No thanks!" laughed Sam. "Let's play pirates!"

They played pirates and dinosaurs and princes and princesses until it was time to go home.

"Do you have any other books about dinosaurs?"
asked Bella.

"Sure!" said Buster.

"What about frogs?" asked Francine.

"Yes," said Buster. "And toads too."

"Anything else about witches and magic?"
asked Max.

"Loads!"

"Can I borrow another pirate story?"
Sam asked.
    "Of course you can,"
laughed Buster, "as long as you promise
not to eat it!"